Author: Casey W. Christofferson

Project Manager: Zach Glazar

Editor: Jeff Harkness

Pathfinder Conversion: Michael "Mars" Russell

Art Direction: Casey Christofferson

Layout and Graphic Design: Charles A. Wright

Cover Design: Charles A. Wright

Cover Art: Adrian Landeros

Interior Art: Adrian Landeros

Cartography: Robert Altbauer

Fantasy Grounds Conversion: Michael G. Potter

Frog God Games is:

Bill Webb, Matthew J. Finch, Zach Glazar, Charles A. Wright, Edwin Nagy, Mike Badolato, John Barnhouse

FROG GOD GAMES

ISBN: 978-1-62283-866-0

TABLE OF CONTENTS

THE TOWER OF JHEDOPHAR

INTRODUCTION

The Tower of Jhedophar is an adventure designed for four to six characters of 13th – 15th level, although it is easily scaled for higher or lower levels with slight modifications. For suggestions on how to scale the adventure, see the **Scaling the Adventure** sidebar. The adventure has several difficult traps that only a skilled rogue may bypass or remove. It is therefore suggested that at least one character be a rogue, and that the party also include one cleric or druid, and one arcane spellcaster. The remainder of the party should consist of frontline fighters or multi-classed characters.

BACKGROUND

The Tower of Jhedophar was once a great school of magic where the arch-mage Jhedophar trained many of the age's greatest wizards and sorcerers in the arcane arts. Times changed — as did Jhedophar — and as the half-elf finally felt the weariness of age creep into his bones, he began frantically to strive as many wizards do for means to unnaturally lengthen his life. Such is the fate of wizards to possess the power to bind planes and the mysteries of existence with words, alchemy, and the secret numbers that are the root of the universe. Vexing it must be to have so many wonders to discover yet only a limited lifespan with which to uncover even greater knowledge.

Jhedophar was once a great hero who, with the aid of Lord Tork and other great heroes, wrested the *mandrake staff* from the witches of Stench-Hollow Downs. Many adventures did he have, the strange *mandrake staff* figuring greatly in the building of his legend, and some say that the fame of his exploits indeed contributed to the success of his school of magic. At some point, however, something changed in Jhedophar, turning his heart to evil. Some say it was the power of the *mandrake staff*, while others claim it was contact with a dark force he discovered while walking the planes of creation.

For whatever reason, 800 years ago, or so the legend says, Jhedophar wrought a great ritual within the summoning chamber of his tower and made contact with a being of pure evil whose will and mind were greater than his own. There, Jhedophar was granted immortality in un-death by the might of this unspeakable power. Jhedophar signed and sealed the pact with the blood of his very own apprentices.

Always fearful of thieves, Jhedophar constructed a great covered labyrinth around the base of his tower, girding it from outside intrusions. This labyrinth that guards the entrance to the tower is nearly as legendary as the tower itself, having been the bane of many a treasure seeker or would-be plunderer of the secrets that Jhedophar hath wrought within his eldritch fortress.

Beyond the construction of the labyrinth and the sealing of the great portal, little is known of what goes on within the gleaming tower. It is believed that Jhedophar is a great traveler of the planes and a frequent visitor to the City of Brass. Speculation being what it is, one fact remains: Jhedophar was the bearer of the *mandrake staff*, a unique staff said to possess unlimited power in the hands of its wielder.

SYNOPSIS

Having heard of the great wonders hidden within the Tower of Jhedophar, the characters seek out the structure to plunder its vast resources of magical knowledge and to destroy the powerful evil which the very existence of Jhedophar represents. The characters travel a great distance through tangled wilderness or over rough and stormy seas (at your discretion) to finally reach the fabled Tower of Jhedophar. Once

there, they enter the Labyrinth of Jhedophar that girds the tower's exterior. The characters face down new adversaries and traps before they enter the tower's forbidden portals and peruse its secrets.

After encountering undead creatures known as **spellgorged zombies**, the characters finally face Jhedophar, where the lich attempts to dissuade them from destroying him by asking the characters to rid him of a red dragon that has taken up residence in his labyrinth. The party may have already made the same deal with the dragon, who is attempting to gain the fabled *mandrake staff* for himself!

Upon completing the adventure, the characters gain a new powerful magic item and knowledge of new magical spells. It is possible the characters may gain the sword known as *Karelis*, a weapon that may be used as a seed for further adventure.

ADVENTURE HOOKS

The characters may find their way to the Tower of Jhedophar by various routes. Since it has no set location, you may insert the Tower of Jhedophar into your campaign wherever you desire. It could be located in an evil city, in a ruin, on an island, in a lost jungle, or high up on a mountaintop. Any wilderness adventures of appropriate difficulty to lead the characters to the tower are your domain. Listed below are adventure hooks designed to get the characters immediately involved in the adventure.

• While traveling from one place to another, the characters discover they are passing close to the Tower of Jhedophar. Appropriate Knowledge (Arcana) checks offer clues about the fall of Jhedophar and the possible secrets hidden within his tower.

• Villagers beseech the characters to seek out and destroy a dragon that is laired within the cursed Tower of Jhedophar. They tell of a band of heroes who went forth over a month ago to slay the dragon but never returned.

• A treasure map describes a fabulous magical item called the *mandrake staff* and its supposed location in a place called the Tower of Jhedophar.

• A cleric character is sent by his religious order to bring back the *mandrake staff* from the clutches of Jhedophar so that its power may be investigated. This plot device works equally well for wizards, who are sent instead by their guild. Alternatively, a wizard's guild could send the characters to seek revenge on Jhedophar for murdering his apprentices.

• A paladin's order, ranger's troupe, or barbarian's clan sends the characters out in search of the lost sword *Karelis* that is said to have belonged to the famed knight known as Lord Tork. The sword is destined to help thwart a great evil soon coming to the world.

THE LABYRINTH OF JHEDOPHAR

The labyrinth of Jhedophar was constructed to keep would-be thieves from bothering his delicate arcane studies. It serves as the lair to his undead minions and protectors such as Nazoj the demiurge and E'elaim the crypt thing. The adult red dragon Exeterus also makes his home here. He is an uninvited squatter residing in the western side of the labyrinth. The characters must navigate this dangerous labyrinth to find the actual entrance to the Tower of Jhedophar, possibly enlisting the aid of the spirits and monsters within the labyrinth to accomplish their goal. Of course, we all know that's not going to happen, and the characters will instead crawl from this adventure covered in blood and gore.

The tower obviously cannot be climbed without magical means. Characters choosing to climb using *spider climb* or who *levitate* or *fly* to the top of the disk note that the roof is broken along the southwestern edge of the disk. The disk is 270 feet in diameter and 20 feet tall, with the tower rising from the center of the disk itself.

The entry portals are solid two-inch-thick bronze and locked with an *arcane lock* spell and a mechanical lock (2 in. thick; Hardness 10; Hp 60; Break DC 38 [28 if *arcane lock* is dispelled], Disable Device DC 35 [25 if *arcane lock* is dispelled]).

L-1. ENTRANCE CHAMBER

THE LABYRINTH OF JHEDOPHAR

Entrances and Exits: Area **L-1** in the south of the tower complex; roof opening in **Area L-11**.

Wandering Monsters: The animated remains of many unlucky adventurers scour much of the labyrinth in search of food. Roll 1d12 once every 30 minutes the characters spend within the labyrinth.

1d12	Encounter
1	1d2 wraiths
2	1d4 + 1 bloody bones
3	1d4 spectres
4	1d2 minotaur ghouls
5	2d4 four-armed gargoyles
6	1d4 barrow wights
7–12	No encounter

Barrow Wight (1d4)   CR 4
XP 1,200
hp 37 (Tome of Horrors Complete, "Wight, Barrow")

Bloody Bones (1d4 + 1)   CR 4
XP 1,200
hp 42 (Tome of Horrors Complete, "Bloody Bones")

Four-Armed Gargoyle (2d4)   CR 5
XP 1,600
hp 57 (Tome of Horrors Complete, "Gargoyle, Four-Armed")

Minotaur Ghoul (1d2)   CR 4
XP 1,200
hp 27 (Appendix B: New Monsters, "Ghoul, Minotaur")

Spectre (1d4)   CR 7
XP 3,200
hp 52 (Pathfinder Roleplaying Game Bestiary, "Spectre")

Wraith (1d2)   CR 5
XP 1,600
hp 47 (Pathfinder Roleplaying Game Bestiary, "Wraith")

Shielding. The labyrinth is shielded from teleportation and dimensional travel into it. However, it is not shielded from teleportation out of the labyrinth. Jhedophar may enter and exit the labyrinth as he pleases, which is to say, he does not, traveling directly to his chambers in his tower and avoiding the goings on within the labyrinth altogether.

Continuous Effects. The entire labyrinth is affected as if by a *desecrate* spell that strengthens the power of the undead creatures dwelling within it. Any creature slain within the labyrinth rises as a bloody bones in 1d6 rounds. If a spellcaster begins to cast *raise dead* or *resurrection* on a slain creature before the 1d6 rounds pass and the spell is successfully completed, the creature does not transform into undead.

Standard Features. Unless otherwise noted, all doors within the labyrinth of Jhedophar are locked and made of two-inch-thick bronze (2 in. thick; Hardness 10; Hp 60; Break DC 28, Disable Device DC 25). Nazoj the demiurge (area **L-10**) and E'elaim the crypt thing (area **L-17**) hold *wardstones of Jhedophar* that open all the doors inside the labyrinth and the tower.

When read, the writing on the wall instantly transforms into a tongue the reader easily comprehends. It says: "Be gone fools who tread within the labyrinth of Jhedophar; from here my tower door is too far. Sad it was the day you chose to invade my home and thus here forever will reside thy bones."

As soon as the characters enter the labyrinth, Jhedophar casts a *wall of iron* over the doorway to block their escape. He has been scrying their progress with his *crystal ball*.

L-2. BLOODY BONES

Five **bloody bones** sit on the floor throwing dice and gambling over a pile of gold coins. They attack when the characters enter the chamber.

Remember to include the effects of the labyrinth's continuous *desecrate* spell on all undead.

Bloody Bones (5)   **CR 4**
XP 1,200
hp 42 (Tome of Horrors Complete, "Bloody Bones")

Treasure: The bloody bones have 300 gp that they have been passing back and forth to one another as they mindlessly gambled away the ages.

L-3. Spiked Pit Trap

Stepping on the floor plate in this corner triggers a locking spiked pit trap. The pit is 10 feet wide by 10 feet long by 20 feet deep.

Spiked Pit Trap   CR 2
XP 600
Type mechanical; **Perception** DC 20; **Disable Device** DC 20
Trigger location; **Reset** automatic (1 minute)
Effect 20-ft.-deep pit (2d6 falling damage); pit spikes (Atk
+10 melee, 1d4 spikes per target for 1d4+2 damage each);
DC 20 Reflex avoids; multiple targets (all targets in a
10-ft.-square area)

L-4. Trapper

A large, ornately carved chest sitting in the center of this broad, irregularly shaped room is a **trapper**. The creature waits until the majority of the party crosses into the center of the room to attack.

Trapper   CR 8
XP 4,800
hp 123 (Pathfinder Roleplaying Game Bestiary 4, "Lurking
Ray, Trapper")

L-5. Ten Pin Alley

Stepping on this trapped floor plate triggers a magical trap set long ago by Jhedophar in one of his crueler moods. The floor plate triggers a *mass hold monster* spell that affects every creature within a 10 ft radius. Within seconds a giant stone ball hidden behind an illusory wall to the north rolls down the hallway crushing all within its path.

***Mass Hold Monster* Trap**   CR 8
XP 4,800
Type magical; **Perception** DC 30; **Disable Device** DC 30
Trigger location; **Reset** automatic (10 minutes)
Effect spell effect (*mass hold monster*, 10 ft radius; Will save
DC 27 negates)

Rolling Boulder Trap   CR 10
XP 9,600
Type mechanical; Perception DC 30; Disable Device DC 25
Trigger location; **Reset** automatic
Effect rolling boulder (12d6 bludgeoning damage; DC 25
Reflex save for half); multiple targets (all targets in the
corridror)

L-6. Crypt of Lord Tork

Rotting tapestries depicting the great deeds of a long-dead warrior hang in this chamber. A large stone sepulcher carved in the likeness of the warrior buried within dominates the room. A glint of shining metal can be spied upon the ground next to the sepulcher, hidden among the remains of a broken armor rack set up to hang the tack and harness of a mighty warhorse.

One round after characters enter the chamber, the sepulcher's lid slides free, and the skeleton warrior that was once **Lord Tork** rises from his tomb. In life, Lord Tork was a great hero, a cavalier without measure among the horsemen of his age. He was also Jhedophar's ally and swore to protect the wizard for all the days of his life. He even granted Jhedophar the land upon which the tower is built. However, Lord Tork never expected the depths to which the wizard's greed and lust for knowledge would take him. When word came that Jhedophar sealed the school and slew his apprentices, Lord Tork rode forth upon his valiant steed Jasper to challenge the wizard.

The vigilant Jhedophar was prepared for the aging hero, however, and slew Lord Tork, binding his soul to a circlet of gold. Jhedophar now controls the poor hero's bones from his scrying chamber, forcing the long-ago hero to serve as a guardian to the wizard's lair.

Remember to include the effects of the labyrinth's continuous *desecrate* spell on all undead.

Lord Tork   CR 17
XP 102,400
hp 120 (Appendix B: New Monsters, "Lord Tork")

Tactics: Lord Tork apologizes for his actions, but attacks the PCs relentlessly and ruthlessly. He makes judicious use of Spring Attack to avoid being ganged up on by the PCs. He is not above using Sunder to destroy missile weapons if he begins taking damage from arrows and crossbows. Lord Tork will attempt to maneuver himself into such a position that he need only face one or two PCs at a time so that he may unleash his deadly blows by making full attacks. As Lord Tork faces his eventual destruction he regains a moment of control and memory of his former life. He bequeaths *Karelis* to his most honorable opponent with the following words. "Take her, and defend her as she defends thee, may you complete the task which I failed."**Note:** If the characters somehow find a way to free Lord Tork from his servitude by gaining the golden circlet from Jhedophar, grant each of them a 1,000 XP story award bonus. Should the characters cast *true resurrection* upon the dust that was once Lord Tork, his ashes rise as a lawful good 16th level fighter in his mid-fifties, to find his stats remove the skeletal warrior template. While wielding the fabled blade *Karelis*, Lord Tork is dashing and brave. Seeing the characters as great and noble allies, he offers to join them in defeating Jhedophar and Exeterus — if they then travel with him to the Plane of Agony to seek the Citadel of the Flayer Knights where *Karelis'* body has been imprisoned for thousands of years.

Treasure: The glinting metal in the chamber is *+2 chain barding* and *horseshoes of a zephyr* that once belonged to Jasper.

What bit of memory still resides within the skull of Lord Tork remembers the sword *Karelis* well and prays that the soul within the blade may someday return to the elf maiden to whom it belongs. Although he attempted to do so in life, it was a quest he would unfortunately never fulfill.

L-7. Entry Hall to the Inner Labyrinth

An **iron golem** guarding the chamber leading to the inner labyrinth animates and attacks the characters instantly.

The portals to the inner labyrinth are 1-foot-thick stone and held with an *arcane lock* spell and locked with a mechanical lock (Hardness 8, HP 90, Break DC 50 [40], Disable Device DC 35 [25]).

Iron Golem CR 13
XP 25,600
hp 129 (Pathfinder Roleplaying Game Bestiary, "Golem, Iron")

L-8. Rue Mohrgs Morgue

This chamber is guarded by 3 **mohrgs** that attack the characters as soon as they enter the chamber. Remember to include the effects of the labyrinth's continuous *desecrate* spell on all undead.

Mohrg (3) CR 8
XP 4,800
hp 91 (Pathfinder Roleplaying Game Bestiary, "Mohrg")

The mohrgs are made up of the bodies of greedy adventurers who sought to wrest the *mandrake staff* from Jhedophar but were destroyed and turned into mohrgs after hours of torture. Their treasures have long since fallen into other hands.

L-9. One Wrong Turn

Stepping upon this floor plate triggers a scything blade trap. Putting more than 20 pounds of pressure on the plate causes three razor sharp blades to emerge from the wall and swipe horizontally across the width of the hallway between 3 and 5 feet off the ground.

Scything Blade Trap CR 5
XP 1,600
Type mechanical; **Perception** DC 20; **Disable Device** DC 20
Trigger location; **Reset** automatic reset
Effect scythes (3 Atk +20 melee, 2d4+6/×4)

L-10. Nazoj's Chamber (or You're Not on the List!)

The demonic trappings of a fallen priest adorn this small chamber, and the ghost-like image of a being twisted with evil rises from the shadows.

This is **Nazoj the demiurge**.

He turns toward any priest or paladin and laughs cruelly. He asks, "So, are you on the list?" The creature looks over a parchment that crumbles to dust in its ghost-like hands. "No. It doesn't appear as if you are on the list after all. Truly too bad for you, but if you aren't on the list, Jhedophar says I have to kill you. I have fallen far in service to Jhedophar. So too shall you fall in the name of our dread queen Beluiri." With that, Nazoj shakes his head and says, "Besides, if you're not on the list, you're just not on the list." He then attacks.

Remember to include the effects of the labyrinth's continuous *desecrate* spell on all undead.

Nazoj the demiurge CR 6
XP 2,400
hp 68 (Tome of Horrors Complete, "Demiurge")

Tactics. The demiurge uses his Transfixing Gaze on heavily armed and armored opponents so that he may use his Soul Touch ability to fly through them and slay them with ease. He next turns his attention to clerics and wizards to finish them off before they can harm him.

A doorway in the eastern wall leads to **Area L-18** of the inner labyrinth.

Treasure. The skeletal remains of three of the demiurge's previous victims bear the following items: a *major ring of energy resistance* (fire), a *cursed chain shirt* that appears as a *+2 chain shirt* but actually grants –2 to the wearer's armor class, a suit of *+2 scale mail*, and the *wardstone of Jhedophar*.

Note: The *wardstone of Jhedophar* allows free passage through the *arcane locked* doors of the Tower of Jhedophar without triggering any of the curses or traps upon them — with the exception of the doors to Jhedophar's personal chambers. Jhedophar left the *wardstone* with the demiurge as he knows Nazoj would give the stone only to someone who knows him well and is on legitimate business.

L-11. Lair of Exeterus

At this point, **Exeterus** the adult red dragon partially reveals himself to the characters. The characters must talk or act quickly, or all is lost. Exeterus, like most of his loathsome kind, is a smart and deadly opponent. Should the characters impress Exeterus with the proper amount of pandering to his might and power, the red dragon makes his play, suggesting that the characters retrieve the *mandrake staff* for him. In return, he shall spare their meager lives.

If asked why he has not simply taken the staff, he scoffs and explains that the mighty lich Jhedophar has been too frightened to come down from his high tower and face the dragon's wrath. This is partially true. Jhedophar does indeed fear Exeterus, for he knows that while he could possibly destroy the dragon, the dragon has better than even odds of destroying him as well. Jhedophar figures that Exeterus makes a good guardian for his labyrinth, and so he simply ignores the upstart dragon. Should the characters agree to destroy Jhedophar and bring Exeterus the *mandrake staff*, the dragon tells them exactly where a pass key for all the doors in the tower and labyrinth is located (a *wardstone of Jhedophar* in **Area L-10** with Nazoj the Demiurge).

Of course, Exeterus has no intention of keeping his part of the bargain. Should the characters destroy Jhedophar, he greedily accepts the staff from them and then attempts to destroy them. Furthermore, should the characters attempt to sneak off without giving him the staff, he stops at nothing to hunt them down until they are destroyed or he is.

Exeterus, the Red Dragon · CR 15
XP 51,200
hp 237 (Appendix B: New Monsters, "Exeterus")

Tactics. The vision the characters see when they enter is not actually Exeterus but a *silent image* that the *invisible* Exeterus stands behind. If the party makes too much noise in **Areas L-12** or **L-13** Exeterus is waiting for them with these spells in place when they arrive.

If the characters arrive looking for a fight, Exeterus breathes upon them. He follows by casting *slow* on lightly armored foes and *charm person* on heavily armored ones. Once he starts taking damage, he continues breathing fire on rounds that he can and focuses on individual targets, seeking to slay one after another until all the characters are dead. Should any attempt to escape, Exeterus casts *scrying* to discern their location and mercilessly hunts them down. If necessary, he casts *charm person* on the party's rogue to get him sneak attacking his buddies instead.

Treasure: Exeterus' treasure hoard contains the following items: a *+4 heavy fortification heavy steel shield*, a *ring of protection +4*, a *cursed ring of wizardry III* that actually reduces the number of third level spells the wearer can use by half, casting illusions in place of the spells that the caster "thinks" they have cast that are only seen by the caster and his allies. There is also a *staff of healing*, a *wand of ice storm* (15 charges), a *+4 greatsword*, a *wand* of *keen edge* (44 charges), a *ring of three wishes* with one *wish* remaining, and a pair of *eyes of petrification*. Exeterus also has 16,000 gp worth of various coins, and 3,450 gp worth of gems, jewelry, and fine art.

L-12. Lartugi's Chamber

Lartugi was once a famous halfling rogue who specialized in raiding and plundering the towers of several wizards throughout the world. That was until he took the left turn upon entering the labyrinth of Jhedophar and came face to face with Exeterus. Now, Lartugi is Exeterus' thrall, valet, and spokesperson when the dragon wishes to be left undisturbed. Exeterus keeps Lartugi constantly under the effects of *charm person* and *suggestion* spells. He gave Lartugi some valuables from his treasure hoard to keep the halfling satisfied.

Lartugi is fairly intelligent but totally in the thrall of his dragon master, whom he defends to the death.

If the party made lots of noise fighting the gargoyles in **Area L-14**, Lartugi hides and sneaks up to just outside **Area L-13** to observe them. Lartugi then slips behind them with his enormous stealth ability and waits for them to meet his master Exeterus. Should the characters fight Exeterus, Lartugi remains in the shadows (and out of the way of Exeterus' breath weapon). If the characters take the deal, he tails them through the maze and tower, possibly aiding them as silently and quietly as he can while they fight Jhedophar.

Lartugi · CR 10
XP 9,600
hp 72 (Appendix B: New Monsters, "Lartugi")

Treasure. Lartugi, a thief through and through, hid his treasure (excluding what he carries on his person) within his chamber under a loose flagstone that requires a success on a DC 30 Perception check to detect. In the hollow under the stone is a bag of gemstones worth 900 gp and a sack with 100 pp in it.

L-13. Watch Your Step

A hidden pit trap lies here. The trap is triggered by the first person to cross over the covering but doesn't activate until another being crosses. Thus, any scouts can pass over it with ease, but those following are in danger.

Covered Pit Trap   CR 3
XP 800
Type mechanical; **Perception** DC 20; **Disable Device** DC 20
Trigger location; **Reset** manual
Effect 60-ft.-deep pit (6d6 falling damage); DC 20 Reflex
    avoids; multiple targets (all targets in a 10-ft.-square area)

A patch of **phycomid** grows upon the bones of a dead rogue at the bottom of the pit. Among the rogue's possessions are a set of masterwork thieves' tools and a *+3 dagger*. The rest of the rogue's armor and equipment have long since rotted away. Casting *speak with dead* upon the rogue reveals that his name was Yadre and that he was a servant of the infamous Underguild. His masters sent him to steal the *mandrake staff* in exchange for a promise of immortality.

Phycomid   CR 4
XP 1,200
hp 39 (Pathfinder Roleplaying Game Bestiary 2, "Phycomid")

The phycomid fires its acid pellet at the first victim to fall into the pit as soon as the creature lands.

L-14. Gargoyles' Lair

This chamber is home to 12 **four-armed gargoyles** and an advanced margoyle known as **Grytis**. The 13 line the walls of the chamber, frozen, making it impossible to notice that the creatures are actually alive. Grytis and his brethren wait until the characters are in the center of the room to attack.

Four-Armed Gargoyle (12)   CR 5
XP 1,600
hp 57 (Tome of Horrors Complete, "Gargoyle, Four-Armed")

Grytis   CR 7
XP 3,200
hp 87 (Appendix B: New Monsters, "Grytis")

Tactics. The gargoyles gang up on individual characters, with three groups of four attacking one character at a time, intent on destroying them. If the party makes lots of noise in **Area L-1**, the gargoyles cover themselves in *adherer oil* that Exeterus gave them. The gargoyles worship Exeterus and make as much noise as they can while fighting. They may even disengage from combat to warn the dragon. For years, a disgusted Jhedophar has attempted to eradicate the gargoyles from the labyrinth's foyer, only to have them return whenever he is off visiting the planes of existence.

L-15. Entrance to the Inner Labyrinth

A pair of **barrow wights** guard the true entrance to the inner labyrinth. The barrow wights immediately attack.

Barrow Wight (2)   CR 4
XP 1,200
hp 37 (Tome of Horrors Complete, "Wight, Barrow")

A hallway to the southeast leads deeper into the labyrinth.

L-16. Death from Above

A pressure plate in the floor triggers a falling block trap. If triggered, the only true path to the labyrinth is permanently sealed off, requiring a *passwall* or similar spell to bypass it.

Falling Block Trap   CR 5
XP 1,600
Type mechanical; **Perception** DC 20; **Disable Device** DC 20
Trigger location; **Reset** manual
Effect Atk +15 melee (10' stone block; 6d6); multiple targets
    (all targets in a 10-ft. square)

L-17. E'elaim's Chamber

Once a sorceress and ally of Jhedophar, the crypt thing that remains is filled with spite and cruelty although she is not necessarily evil. **E'elaim** is bound to the power of Jhedophar for all eternity. She sits upon a throne fit for a queen, carved from brilliantly polished vermillion wood inlaid with gold and precious jewels. She uses her powers of teleportation to cast intruders from the entrance of Jhedophar's tower as she clacks her dusty jaws in a mockery of laughter.

Remember to include the effects of the labyrinth's continuous *desecrate* spell on all undead.

TELEPORT LOCATIONS

When E'elaim teleports a character, roll 1d20 on the table below to see where the target ends up. This result could prove quite deadly to characters, so handle the encounter with care.

1d20	Location
1	Area L-1. Entrance Chamber
2	Area L-2. Bloody Bones
3	Area L-3. Spiked Pit Trap
4	Area L-4. Trapper
5	Area L-5. Ten Pin Alley
6	Area L-6. Crypt of Lord Tork
7	Area L-7. Entry Hall to the Inner Labyrinth
8	Area L-8. Rue Mohrgs Morgue
9	Area L-9. One Wrong Turn
10	Area L-10. Nazoj's Chamber
11	Area L-11. Lair of Exeterus
12	Area L-12. Lartugi's Chamber
13	Area L-13. Watch Your Step
14	Area L-14. Gargoyles' Lair
15	Area L-15. Entrance to the Inner Labyrinth
16	Area L-16. Death from Above
17	Outside the labyrinth
18	Area L-18. False Entrance to the Tower
19	Area L-19. Crypts of the Barrow Wights
20	Area L-20. Shadow and Shadow Rats' Nests

E'elaim the crypt thing CR 5
XP 1,600
hp 52 (Pathfinder Roleplaying Game Bestiary 2, "Crypt Thing")

Tactics. E'elaim attempts to teleport creatures within 50 feet of her in random directions throughout the labyrinth. She then flees into the tower to avoid the characters' subsequent assault, laughing hysterically all the while.

Treasure. The throne that the crypt thing sits upon is made of precious hardwoods and gold. It weighs just over 70 pounds and is worth approximately 700 gp to a collector in a large city. E'elaim also holds a *wardstone of Jhedophar* that she created.

Note: The *wardstone of Jhedophar* allows free passage through the *arcane locked* doors of the Tower of Jhedophar without triggering any of the curses or traps upon them — with the exception of the doors to Jhedophar's personal chambers.

L-18. False Entrance to the Tower

The doorway to this chamber is ornately wrought bronze and gives the impression that it is an antechamber leading to the foot of the Tower of Jhedophar. Halls lead off to the north and south, obviously skirting the tower itself. Many wards are scribed upon the portal, and a character making a successful DC 28 Knowledge (Arcana) or Perception check can discover that the door is warded with a permanent *magic circle against evil*.

Inscribed above the door is a warning that reads: "Turn ye back from the Tower of Jhedophar, or face his wrath. Let one thousand curses blister your carcasses and burn your soul to ash and soot, and a thousand years may you suffer in torment for defiling his home! Be gone thieves this is thy last warning!"

This chamber beyond the doorway is the lair of **Clytos the gharros demon**. Beluiri gifted Clytos to Jhedophar as punishment when the gharros demon fell into her disfavor. Rather than destroy Clytos, she sent him to Jhedophar to do with as he wished. Of course, Clytos was recalcitrant and lazy. Having little use for Clytos other than as a guardian in his labyrinth, Jhedophar exiled the gharros demon to live within this chamber.

The wizard sealed the door with a special *magic circle against evil* and *bestow curse* trap. Fiddling with the door breaks the *magic circle* and triggers the *bestow curse* (DC 24) upon the fool tampering with the doorway.

Bestow Curse Trap CR 5
XP 1,600
Type magical; **Perception** DC 30; **Disable Device** DC 30
Trigger touch; **Reset** automatic
Effect spell effect (*bestow curse* CL 5, -6 penalty to Dexterity, DC 24 Will save negates)

Clytos survived all these years by summoning lesser demons and devouring them when they found themselves trapped within the *magic circle*.

Clytos bears a large *+3 unholy battleaxe of mighty cleaving* named *Suzette* that he wields with deadly efficiency. He named the battleaxe in honor of the erinyes that Beluiri caught him with at a social event in the lower planes. Once the circle is broken, the demon intends to slay whomever he can in his rage at his long imprisonment. He does not leave the labyrinth, however; he knows that Jhedophar is likely to destroy him for doing so.

Clytos, the gharros demon CR 14
XP 36,400
hp 248 (Tome of Horrors Complete, "Demon, Gharros")

Add +3 to hit and damage with the battleaxe to reflect *Suzette's* power.

L-19: Crypts of the Barrow Wights

This chamber holds the crypts of 6 **barrow wights** who were Lord Tork's liegemen. They came to rescue his body from Jhedophar's clutches but failed miserably and now rest here as guardians.

Each barrow wight wears masterwork plate armor and has a *+1 greatsword* that it leaves inside its crypt. They emerge and attack as soon as characters enter.

Remember to include the effects of the labyrinth's continuous *desecrate* spell on all undead.

Barrow Wight (6) CR 4
XP 1,200
hp 37 (Tome of Horrors Complete, "Wight, Barrow")

Change AC to 26, Change Speed to 20

L-20: Shadow and Shadow Rats Nest

This chamber contains a refuse heap that once housed a large colony of dire rats. A **shadow** sent by Jhedophar to clean the labyrinth of any vermin eventually stumbled upon the rats' lair. Now, the **shadow** and his pack of **shadow rats** — along with his 2 spawned **shadows** — wait in the darkness for their next meal. Feasting is good every few years when another foolish party of adventurers attempts to learn the secrets of the tower.

The dire shadow rats and the shadows attack when the characters enter the chamber.

Remember to include the effects of the labyrinth's continuous *desecrate* spell on all undead.

Shadow (3) CR 3
XP 800
hp 19 (Pathfinder Roleplaying Game Bestiary, "Shadow")

Shadow Rat (8) CR 1/2
XP 200
hp 5 (Tome of Horrors Complete, "Shadow Rat")

Treasure. Hidden among the detritus is a *+1 greataxe*, a *potion of cure light wounds*, and 344 gp.

The Tower of Jhedophar

The following locations are found inside the wizard's tower at the center of the labyrinth.

1-A. The Entryway

The front door of the tower is one-foot-thick stone and held with an *arcane lock* spell (Hardness 8, HP 90, Break DC 50 [40]). Hateful runes warn would-be thieves and trespassers away from the door.

Knock suppresses the *arcane lock* but does not protect the caster from the door's curse. Tampering with the door triggers a special *bestow curse* trap (DC 24).

Bestow Curse Trap CR 5
XP 1,600
Type magical; **Perception** DC 30; **Disable Device** DC 30
Trigger touch; **Reset** automatic
Effect spell effect (*bestow curse* CL 18, -6 penalty to Wisdom, DC 24 Will save negates)

Inside the Tower

Wandering Monsters. No wandering monsters are in the Tower of Jhedophar unless the characters let them in from the labyrinth. Instead, roll 1d10 for each level of the tower that the party enters. On a roll of 1, Jhedophar is somewhere upon that level of the tower going about his business. If the characters trigger an *alarm* spell (see **Area 1-B**) alerting Jhedophar, he will be waiting in **Area 2**.

Shielding. The Tower of Jhedophar is shielded from teleportation and dimensional travel into it. However, the shielding does not prevent teleportation out of the tower. Jhedophar may enter and exit the tower as he pleases,. The exterior walls are further shielded to be immune to the effects of *passwall*, *stone shape*, and similar spells. Casting such spells inside the tower is fine, but they do not work on the walls of the outer tower.

Continuous Effects. Due to the shrine to Beluiri, the tower is affected as if by a *desecrate* spell that strengthens the power of the undead creatures dwelling within it.

Standard Features. Unless otherwise noted, all doors within the Tower of Jhedophar are locked and made of bronze (2 in. thick; Hardness 10; Hp 60; Break DC 28, Disable Device DC 25). Nazoj the demiurge (area **L-10**) and E'elaim the crypt thing (area **L-17**) hold *wardstones of Jhedophar* that open all the doors in the labyrinth and the tower (with the exception of the lich's quarters on the eighth floor).

The entry chamber features a portrait of Jhedophar as he appeared in life. He is dressed in his caster's robes and bears a great staff carved in a grotesque and twisted mockery of a man. Several non-magical books are on a small coffee table, and a moldy green sofa and chairs sit around it. The chamber has no windows, and a doorway leads to the north. Several inches of dust coat the sofa, chairs, and the coffee table.

1-B. The Abjuration Chamber

The first floor of the tower is a room dedicated to the school of abjuration, a guard against any who would attempt to bypass Jhedophar's normal protections.

Practitioners once studied spells here, but the thick dust on the floor indicates that such studies must surely have given way to the passage of time and neglect.

Runes are scribed on nearly every surface within this room, upon the tables and walls. Rune bindings and other symbols of protection and wards decorate scroll cases and bookshelves.

Unwarily perusing any of these volumes triggers *pain strike* (DC 22) upon the reader.Two rounds after characters enter the abjuration chamber, 2 **spellgorged zombies** step from the corners of the chamber and unleash a pair of *cone of cold* spells before closing for melee.

Remember to include the effects of the tower's continuous *desecrate* spell on all undead.

Spellgorged Zombie (2)   CR 3
XP 800
hp 27 (Tome of Horrors Complete, "Zombie, Spellgorged")

spell storing (5 levels; cone of cold [15d6, Ref DC 27 half])

Pain Strike **Trap**   CR 3
XP 800
Type magical; **Perception** DC 27; **Disable Device** DC 27
Trigger touch (books); **Reset** automatic
Effect spell effect (*pain strike* CL 18, 1d6 nonlethal per round for 10 rounds plus sickened, DC 22 Fort save negates)

A scroll case holds an *alarm* spell that notifies Jhedophar if it is touched. After scrying on the characters in the labyrinth with his *crystal ball*, Jhedophar assumed they were dealt with and went about his studies. Once he learns the characters breached his tower, however, Jhedophar immediately prepares to face them. He teleports to the evocation chamber (**Area 2**) and prepares to face the intruders.

One scroll case is a *scroll case of obscuring*. Within it are *arcane scrolls* containing the following spells:

Scroll #1: *shield, hold portal, endure elements* **Scroll #2:** *obscure object, protection from arrows* **Scroll #3:** *dispel magic* (CL 5)

Other scrolls and tomes are filled with magical knowledge that references the school of abjuration and its uses. Carefully studying these books (requiring weeks of diligent research equal to 6 minus the character's Intelligence modifier [min 1 week]) grants the reader a permanent +2 circumstance bonus to Knowledge (Arcana) and Spellcraft checks as they pertain to the casting of or use of abjuration spells.

A staircase leads to a warded doorway that opens onto the second floor. The staircase is guarded with a message on the door to all that would intrude upon Jhedophar's stronghold: *Read in me and be relieved! Jhedophar has no time for thieves! With these words shall you burn. For your ashes, I have an urn.*

Reading this warning immediately sets off the *explosive runes* (DC 23) on the door. It can be noticed without setting it off with a successful DC 28 Perception check. The use of *dispel magic* or similar spell (DC 29) may also disable the *runes*.

2. Evocation Chamber

The evocation chamber is a bare room with a sand pit flanked by two low 10-foot-high-by-40-foot-long walls lined with engraved silver runes. Jhedophar created illusions here for those studying evocation spells so that they could practice their skills at arcane combat. He often created encounters for novices similar to what they might encounter on an adventure, thus allowing his apprentices to blast it out in the relative safety of this room. The walls are guarded against magic so that an accidentally miscast spell does not blow debris out into the well-tended flower gardens he once kept on the roof of the labyrinth.

As the characters search the room, a pair of **spellgorged zombies** attack, blasting the party with a pair of *empowered fireballs* (DC 23).

Remember to include the effects of the tower's continuous *desecrate* spell on all undead.

Spellgorged Zombie (2)   CR 3
XP 800
hp 27 (Tome of Horrors Complete, "Zombie, Spellgorged")

Effect spell storing (5 levels; *empowered fireball* [15d6, Ref DC 25 half])

After the fireballs explode, the zombies move forward and attack with their claws until destroyed.

The low walls flanking the sand pit are trapped with *programmed illusion* spells (DC 26). For every 10-foot section crossed, the traps generate the image of a huge fire elemental. Up to 4 such illusions may be generated in this manner. Thus, a character who crosses 30 feet of the sand pit triggers 3 *programmed illusions* of **fire elementals**.

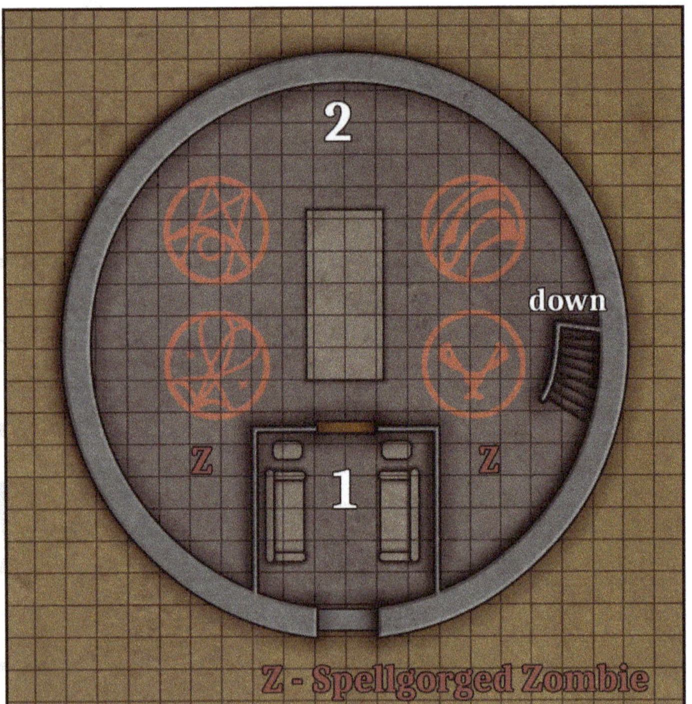

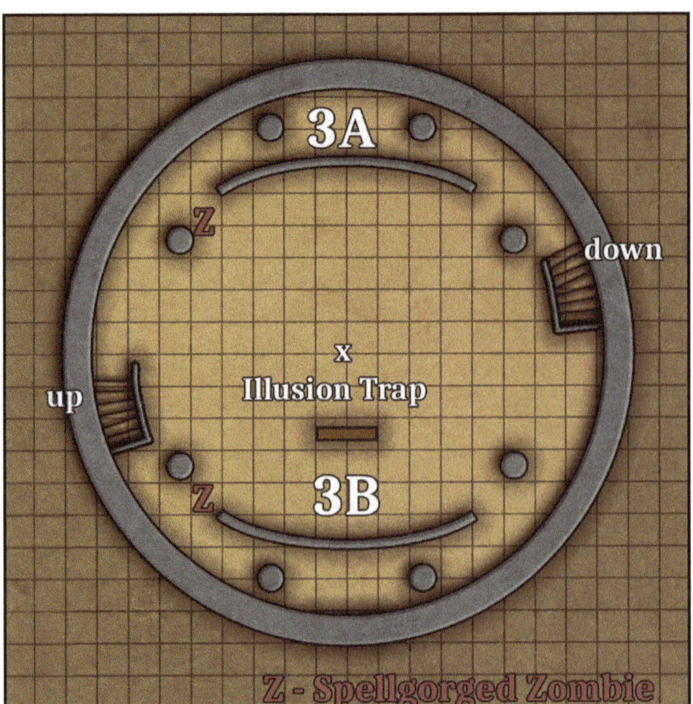

Programmed Image **Trap**   CR 7
XP 3,200
Type magical; **Perception** DC 31; **Disable Device** DC 31
Trigger location; **Reset** automatic
Effect spell effect (*programmed image* CL 18, DC 26 Will
negates)

The staircase in the eastern side of the chamber leads down to the first level. The staircase on the western side leads to the tower's third level.

A staircase around the edge of the room leads to a door on the third floor. It is magically locked and warded, as are all the doors in the tower.

3-A. The Chamber of Illusions

The first task a practitioner of illusions learned from Jhedophar was to tell the difference between illusion and reality. To that end, Jhedophar constructed an illusionary maze on this floor of his tower. Apprentices traced their way through the illusory walls to find the staircase leading up to the tower's fourth floor.

Upon entering the chamber of illusions, 2 **spellgorged zombies** stalk the characters through the maze, ignoring any walls as they are immune to illusions. One of the zombies casts *cloudkill* before closing to slam opponents with its fists. The other casts *confusion* followed by *magic missile*.

Remember to include the effects of the tower's continuous *desecrate* spell on all undead.

Spellgorged Zombie   CR 3
XP 800
hp 27 (Tome of Horrors Complete, "Zombie, Spellgorged")

spell storing (5 levels; confusion [Will DC 24 negates], magic
missile [5 missiles, 1d4])

Spellgorged Zombie   CR 3
XP 800
hp 27 (Tome of Horrors Complete, "Zombie, Spellgorged")

spell storing (5 levels; cloudkill [Fort DC 25 partial])

3-B. False Staircase

Jhedophar created a partial staircase along the western edge of the chamber of illusions. It extends upward about 20 feet with the rest being a permanent *silent image* (DC 21) of a staircase continuing up to the fourth floor. A character following the illusory stairs is considered to be interacting with them. If the character fails to disbelieve the illusion, they must succeed on a DC 20 Reflex saving throw or fall the 20 feet to the floor below, suffering 2d6 bludgeoning damage. Upon landing, a *massacre* trap (DC 29) is cast on the fallen victim.

Massacre **Trap**   CR 7
XP 3,200
Type magical; **Perception** DC 31; **Disable Device** DC 31
Trigger contingency (falling from the top of the staircase);
Reset automatic
Effect spell effect (*massacre* CL 18, DC 29 Will save negates)

4. The Chamber of Enchantments

This floor has two rooms.

4-A. Still the Prettiest

This room is filled with mirrors and paintings, tapestries and murals. One mirror is a *mirror of charming*. Since all the mirrors reflect one another, anyone looking into a mirror must succeed on a DC 20 Will saving throw or become infatuated with his or her own image and be unable leave the mirror's presence. Such creatures merely stand transfixed, brushing their hair and reciting such phrases as "Still the prettiest," or "My, but aren't I a fine one?" characters may make an additional DC 20 Will saving throw if anyone tries to pull them away from staring at their image. On a failure, they become enraged and attack their allies. Each such creature may repeat the saving throw at the end of each of its turns while in combat, ending the effect on itself on a success.

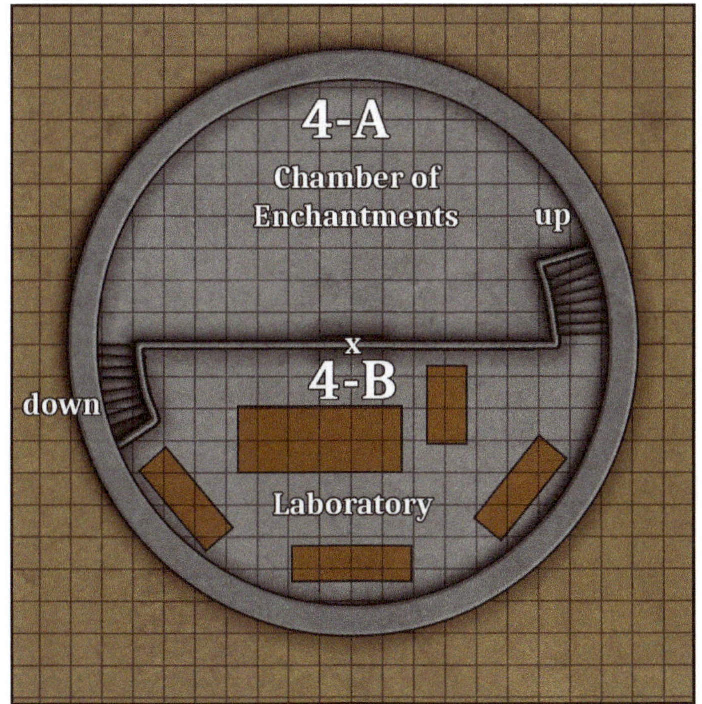

The chamber contains various bones and dust-covered equipment of adventurers who starved to death in front of the mirrors. Standing in front of one of the mirrors is a dwarf whose beard has grown so long that it curls upon the floor. He is so covered in dust that he appears to be a marble statue, requiring a character to succeed on a DC 25 Perception check to notice that he is actually alive.

Imbo the Undying was sent to the Tower of Jhedophar some years ago on behalf of his benefactors to retrieve the *mandrake staff*. While Imbo is a thoroughly evil dwarf, he may assist the characters should they break the enchantment upon him.

If freed, he helps the party up until Jhedophar is destroyed then betrays them at the first opportunity he gets to gain the *mandrake staff* for himself. Of course, in his berserk rage at being pulled away from the *mirror of charming*, he may "accidentally" kill someone. If asked how he managed to survive so long without food or water, Imbo points to a magical ring on his finger and explains that it is an *ring of sustenance*. While using it, he says, he didn't need to eat, drink, or sleep. He is lying, and the ring is actually a *ring of mind shielding*.

Roleplaying Notes. Imbo is as ruthless and bloodthirsty as it gets. Due to a particular curse upon his wretched soul, he cannot truly die, as none of the gods of the heavens or the dukes of Hell will tolerate his despicable presence among them for more than a moment. Even if disintegrated or reduced to ashes by the flames of a dragon, his essence remains and slowly reforms over time. He eventually returns — with slight gaps in his memory — as a stout and cruel dwarf. The reformed Imbo always seeks out the same style of weapons and gear, and always joins up with the cruelest and most powerful of allies. Imbo is an accomplished thief and liar, and takes great pains to conceal his deceptions from the characters until the very last moment when he springs one of his particularly vile traps upon them.

Imbo the Undying   CR 13
XP 25,600
hp 133 (Appendix B: New Monsters, "Imbo the Undying")

Treasure. A successful DC 20 Perception check of the bones and rotting equipment uncovers 1d4 random masterwork weapons, and 2d100 gp. Jhedophar long ago gathered any magical items or gems from these failed intruders.

4-B. LABORATORY

The second room within the chamber of enchantments is an alchemical laboratory with more than 2000 gp worth of masterwork alchemical equipment that grants the user a +4 circumstance bonus to Craft (Alchemy) checks . Several potions and bottles of unguents and reagents are found within this room. It is guarded by an **invisible stalker** that immediately attacks.

Invisible Stalker   CR 7
XP 3,200
hp 80 (Pathfinder Roleplaying Game Bestiary, "Invisible Stalker")

Treasure. Also found within this room are a *potion of suggestion*, a *potion of glibness*, *potion of blink*, and a *potion of poison*.
A staircase leads upward to the next floor.

5. THE CHAMBER OF TRANSMUTATION

Jhedophar works out some of the most complicated forms of magic here, changing one object or item into another. The chamber is filled with benches and tables laden with items such as lead coins, small amounts of gold, rare gems, and the like. Several small cages and a large barred cell are in the corner of the room. The cages contain various creatures such as dire rats and pigeons. Several tools and gears are found in this workshop. If gathered, the tools are of masterwork quality and valued at 1,000 gp.

A **shield guardian** attacks any unbidden intruder entering the chamber of transmutation.

The shield guardian is programmed to trigger a *confusion* spell (DC 24) and then pummel to a pulp anyone attempting to cause it harm. If the shield guardian loses more than 50% of its hit point maximum, it is programmed to flee to Jhedophar's chamber of divination (**Area 8A**).

Shield Guardian   CR 8
XP 4,800
hp 64 (Appendix B: New Monsters, "Golem, Wood Shield Guardian")

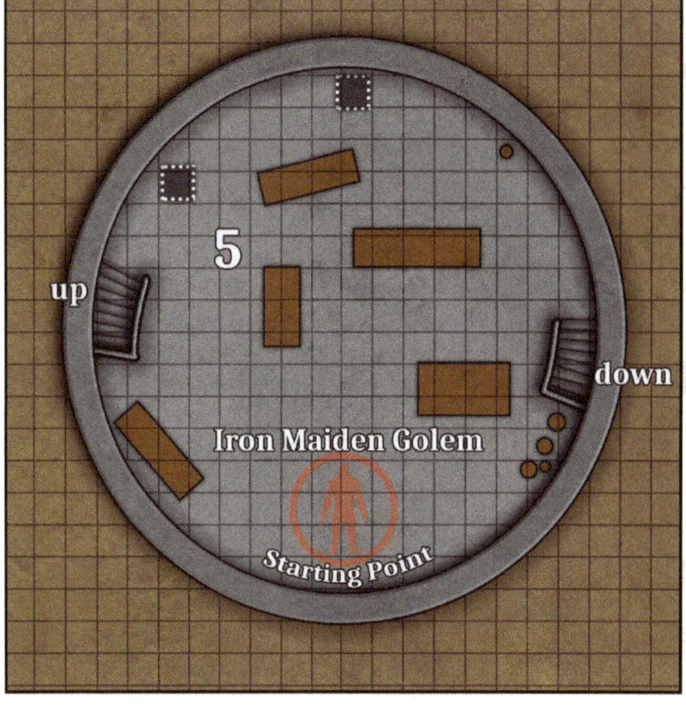

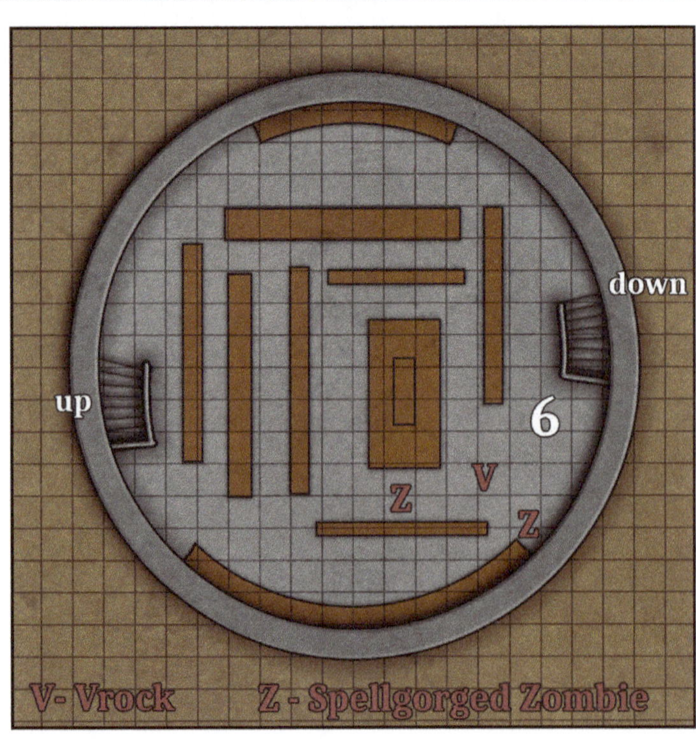

A wand sits on a table. Beside it is a set of scales with a pile of gold and gems on one side and lead coins serving as a counterweight. *Detect magic* reveals the wand is magical, but it is actually trapped with a *baleful polymorph* trap.

Baleful Polymorph Trap   **CR 6**
XP 2,400
Type magical; **Perception** DC 30; **Disable Device** DC 30
Trigger touch (wand); **Reset** automatic
Effect spell effect (*baleful polymorph* CL 18, DC 25 Fort/
  Will negates, anyone failing their saving throw is instantly
  polymorphed into a sheep wearing a blue dress)

The wand is non-magical but detects as magical because of a *magic aura* cast upon it to make it appear as if it is a *wand of polymorph*.

A staircase leads upward to a locked door that is the entryway to the sixth floor.

6. Chamber of Necromancy

Upon entering this chamber, the characters find themselves face to face with a **vrock** flanked by a pair of **spellgorged zombies**. The vrock and zombies attack the party instantly with spells and spell-like abilities before closing in with melee attacks.

Tactics. In the first round of combat, the vrock uses its Stunning Screech ability and the spellgorged zombies unleash their spells. The spellgorged zombies attack by casting *enervation* targeted on a lightly armored opponent, both at the same target. On the second round, the spellgorged zombies attack by casting *ray of enfeeblement* targeted at heavily armored opponents, at different targets this time. Afterwards, the spellgorged zombies move to engage enemies. On the second round, the vrock moves in and uses its Spores ability upon the characters. The vrock and the zombies gang up on one target at a time until destroyed or until they defeat the characters.

Remember to include the effects of the tower's continuous *desecrate* spell on all undead.

Vrock	**CR 9**

XP 6,400
hp 112 (Pathfinder Roleplaying Game Bestiary, "Demon, Vrock")

Spellgorged Zombie (2)	**CR 3**

XP 800
hp 27 (Tome of Horrors Complete, "Zombie, Spellgorged")

Effect: spell storing (5 levels; *enervation, ray of enfeeblement* [1d6+5, Fort DC 21 halves])

In life, Jhedophar was no fan of necromantic magic. However, since becoming a lich, Jhedophar has become a master of all things undead, even raising the bodies of his former apprentices as a new form of undead servant, the spellgorged zombie. Jhedophar taught initiates only necromantic spells that offered defensive possibilities and then only to a select and trusted few. All of this changed when Jhedophar dreamed of a beautiful temptress offering him immortality. He pored over his many eldritch tomes and finally sought out eternal life in un-death when he felt age creep into his bones.

Books and scrolls about the necromantic arts and defenses against the powers of the undead line the walls of this chamber, which is more of a library or a study than any other chamber in the tower. A character studying the tomes collected here for weeks of diligent research equal to 6 – the character's Intelligence modifier [minimum of 1 week] gains a permanent +2 circumstance bonus to any Knowledge (Arcana) checks concerning undead creatures and spells from the school of necromancy.

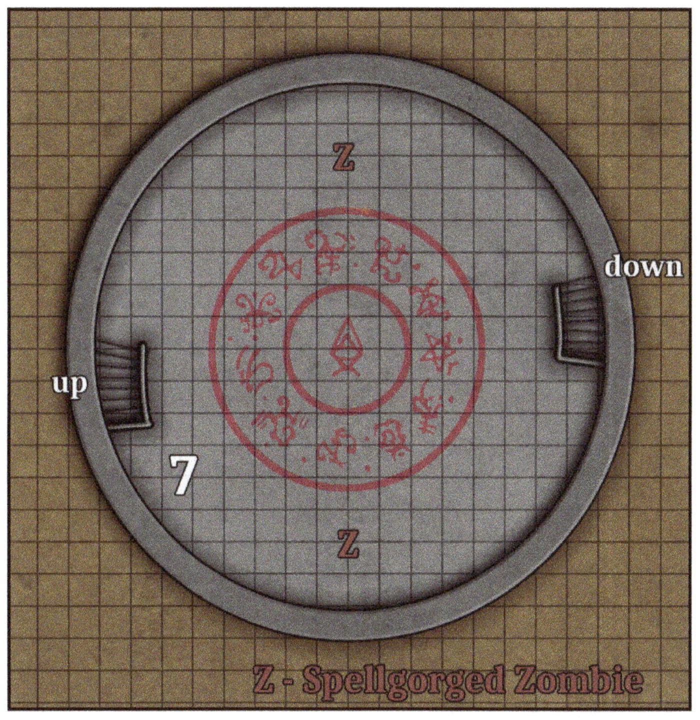

Treasure. A character succeeding on a DC 25 Perception check gleans three *arcane scrolls* of value:

Scroll #1. *halt undead, ray of enfeeblement*, and *gentle repose*
Scroll #2. *ghoul touch, vampiric touch* and *ennervation*
Scroll #3. *spectral hand, create greater undead*, and *animate dead*

7. The Chamber of Conjuration

Binding runes are inscribed on the walls, doors, and floor of this chamber. Only high adepts were allowed entrance to this chamber where Jhedophar conferred with extraplanar forces in his magical research.

Guarding the chamber are 2 **spellgorged zombies** triggered to destroy anyone who enters the chamber unbidden.

Tactics. The first spellgorged zombie casts *cloudkill* while the second summons *black tentacles* near heavily armored characters.

Remember to include the effects of the tower's continuous *desecrate* spell on all undead.

Spellgorged Zombie	**CR 3**

XP 800
hp 27 (Tome of Horrors Complete, "Zombie, Spellgorged")

Effect: spell storing (5 levels; *black tentacles, magic missile* [5 missiles, 1d4])

Spellgorged Zombie	**CR 3**

XP 800
hp 27 (Tome of Horrors Complete, "Zombie, Spellgorged")

Effect: spell storing (5 levels; *cloudkill* [Fort DC 25 partial])

A large magic circle is inscribed on the floor in the center of this chamber. Anyone crossing the threshold of the magical circle triggers a *magic mouth* that utters a curse in Common in Jhedophar's raspy voice: *"Curious of magic, are you? Magic is a force to fear! Your courage fails you in the face of the arcane!"* Any character that can hear the voice and who understands Common must succeed on a DC 26 Will saving throw or be affected by a *mass suggestion* spell which lasts 18 hours. Affected creatures run in terror from anyone or anything perceived to be using arcane magical powers.

***Mass Suggestion* Trap**	**CR 8**

XP 4,800
Type magical; **Perception** DC 30; **Disable Device** DC 30
Trigger location; **Reset** automatic (1 minute)
Effect spell effect (*mass suggestion*, Will save DC 26 negates; multiple targets [all creatures who hear and understand the *magic mouth*])

A staircase leads to the next floor of the tower. A locked and warded door enters the eighth floor.

Treasure. A *brazier of conjuring fire elementals* filled with brimstone sits in the center of a magic circle. If Jhedophar is within his chamber of divination (**Area 8**), he can cause the fire to light and summon a **huge fire elemental**. The elemental throws its support in with the spellgorged zombies.

Huge Fire Elemental	**CR —**

XP —
hp 85 (Pathfinder Roleplaying Game Bestiary, "Elemental, Fire [Huge]")

8-A. THE CHAMBER OF DIVINATION

This floor of the tower holds Jhedophar's private quarters. It is also where Jhedophar uses his *crystal ball* to spot troubles around the world and to seek the deeper mysteries of the universe from within and without the realms of existence. This special divination chamber is for Jhedophar alone to use; apprentices were never allowed entry here due to the level of concentration required for deep scrying. The room is filled with soft throw pillows and draped with velvet curtains. Several *gems of seeing* are on the pillows, and a large *crystal ball* sits on a gilt golden pedestal in the center of the room. A door to the north leads to Jhedophar's private quarters. Jhedophar placed a permanent rune of *nondetection* upon the ceiling of this chamber to allow him to scry freely without worrying about being seen by others.

Unless already encountered elsewhere, **Jhedophar** finally reveals himself to the characters when they reach this room. He stands ominously before the characters, his bony hands clasped around the twisted length of the *mandrake staff*.

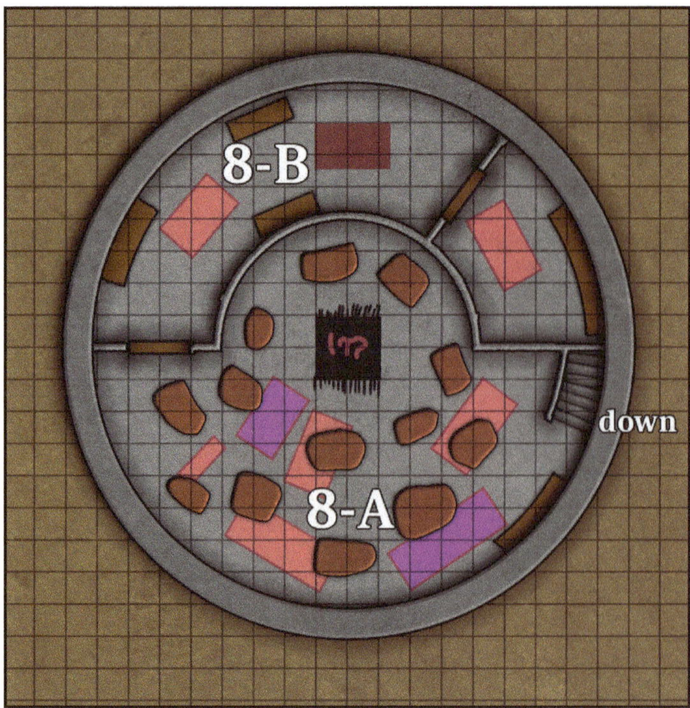

> This lush chamber is filled with plush pillows and shrouded in velvet curtains. Gems gleam from their place on the pillows, and a crystal ball reflects the light. A powerful-looking man stands on the far side of the room, his bony hands clasped around the twisted length of a wooden staff.
>
> *"My name is Jhedophar, and you must be powerful indeed if you seek to steal this twisted staff of root and flesh from me. But think first what you could gain instead if you wait a moment and listen to my parley."*

If characters wait and listen to him, Jhedophar explains that the tower, the staff, and even all the treasures within his tower are worthless compared to his knowledge gained through centuries of researching the occult. In fact, he has grown tired of constantly defending the tower and is arranging to leave it altogether for a new place that is "a bit roomier" with a "more pleasant view."

But, Jhedophar explains, he has no intention of just "giving away" his belongings. He points out that a red dragon named Exeterus is now a squatter in the bowels of the labyrinth. If the characters are brave enough, they may be able to overcome the dragon, in which case he promises to give the tower to the characters. Jhedophar purposely does not mention the *mandrake staff* when he offers to hand over the tower. He has no intention of willingly giving up the staff. However, Jhedophar is very intelligent and understands that a large force of adventurers powerful enough to survive the traps and beasts within his lair may well be able to harm or even slay him.

Beside Jhedophar is a carved statuette of Beluiri sitting on his personal altar to his dark queen. The altar and statuette are hidden beneath a drapery of pure black silk that he keeps over them when entertaining "living" guests. The statuette is enchanted with a *symbol of stunning*, triggered when viewed by any living creature (see Tactics below). The altar of Beluiri is a foul and truly evil set piece to this otherwise lavish chamber. Jhedophar sacrificed each of his apprentices upon this altar and turned them into spellgorged zombies. The altar is under the influence of permanent *desecrate* (which benefits Jhedophar) and *unhallow* spells. Jhedophar cannot be turned while in its presence.

If characters attack (or if they reject his request), he targets the characters with as many deadly spells as possible from his extensive repertoire before casting *plane shift* and making his way to his new fortress upon the Plane of Molten Skies. He plans to work as an ambassador and spy for his dread Queen Beluiri.

Jhedophar   **CR 19**
XP 204,800
hp 189 (Appendix B: New Monsters, "Jhedophar")

Tactics. Jhedophar has had plenty of time to prepare for the characters and already cast several defensive spells by the time the characters enter the divination chamber. Specifically, he has cast *blur, mirror image, resist energy, protection from energy, magic circle against chaos,* and *contingency* (if he is reduced to 25% of his maximum hit points or less, *dimension door* will transport him to a safe location where he can *plane shift* to the Plane of Molten Skies). Rather than destroy the chamber, Jhedophar first casts *mass suggestion* to once again try to get all the characters to sit down on the floor and listen to him. If any still fail to hear him out, he sees no recourse but to destroy them and uses a free action to remove the cover from the altar, unleashing the *symbol of stunning*. He then casts *time stop* and takes the following actions while it is effect. On his first turn, he casts *delayed blast fireball*, targeting a point that will encompass the greatest number of characters but not himself. This should not interfere with the *time stop* as he has not affected another creature… yet. He sets the duration on the *delayed blast fireball* to long as the *time stop* lasts. If he has turns to spare during his *time stop*, he will use the *mandrake staff*'s Walk of the Mandrake ability (instructing it to use its Withering and other attacks on a lightly armored character as soon as *time stop* ends) and use an *arcane scroll* to cast *disintegrate* on a 20-foot square section of the tower floor under characters' feet. Jhedophar then attempts to use an *arcane scroll* to cast *wall of iron* to isolate himself from any remaining physical threats. When *time stop* ends, the *delayed blast fireball* goes off, and anyone standing on the disintegrated floor falls 20' to the seventh level of the tower. He attempts to to keep characters at bay, dropping them and pelting the characters with offensive spells, including *meteor swarm* from an *arcane scroll*.

If the characters severely injure Jhedophar, he *dimension doors* away automatically via his *contingency* spell, recalls the *mandrake staff* to his hand if necessary, and *plane shifts* out of the tower to his new fortress in the Plane of Molten Skies — unless prevented by magical means such as an *antimagic field*.

Note. At your discretion, Lartugi may step in to assist the characters if he was not slain previously. Alternately, if the characters are having too easy of a time with Jhedophar, Lartugi could join the fray as a wild card. If Lartugi still lives and Imbo is with the characters, Imbo switches sides, and he and Lartugi fight Jhedophar and the characters to gain the staff.

Consequences. If Jhedophar escapes, the characters might find themselves in a predicament if they previously made a deal with Exeterus. The red dragon most certainly expects the characters to return the *mandrake staff* to him or to be destroyed trying. They must either kill the dragon, or chase Jhedophar through the planes of existence, destroy him, and retrieve the staff lest Exeterus stalk them for the rest of their lives.

Treasure. 6 *gems of seeing* and a *crystal ball with detect thoughts.* The golden pedestal on which the crystal ball sits is worth 1,390 gp.

Note. The *gems of seeing* work perfectly for Jhedophar should he choose to cast *magic jar* or *trap the soul.*

8-B. Jhedophar's Private Chamber

Jhedophar's bedchamber contains a writing table with enough ink to scribe 20 levels worth of pages in spellbooks. Enough material spell components are in vials and jars here to cast each spell in his spellbooks six times. A locked secret door is behind an illusory wall. The door is guarded by *explosive runes* (DC 23) that read "Look up!" and a falling block trap.

Falling Block Trap   **CR 5**
XP 1,600
Type mechanical; **Perception** DC 20; **Disable Device** DC 20
Trigger location; **Reset** manual
Effect Atk +15 melee (10' stone block; 6d6); multiple targets
    (all targets in a 10-ft. square)

A small chamber beyond the trapped door holds a staff, several robes, and a bookshelf that contains many different dusty volumes. Scroll cases line the top of the shelves, and a silver dagger hangs from a chain upon a hook.

A character making a successful DC 30 Perception check discovers an *invisible* bookshelf that contains Jhedophar's actual spellbooks. The other books are each enchanted with *magic aura* to appear magical and trapped with *pain strike.* They are filled with confusing gibberish; Jhedophar cast *illusory script* on them to fool common thieves into thinking they are of great value. They merely confuse a spellcaster attempting to read them as if they were under the effects of a *confusion* spell (DC 24).

***Pain Strike* Trap**   **CR 3**
XP 800
Type magical; **Perception** DC 27; **Disable Device** DC 27
Trigger touch (books); **Reset** automatic
Effect spell effect (*pain strike* CL 18, 1d6 nonlethal per round
    for 10 rounds plus sickened, DC 22 Fort save negates)

Treasure. Jhedophar's spellbooks. These large volumes are covered in *illusory script.* Perusing them gives the impression that they are blank. Characters also find a solid silver *+2 keen dagger*, a **flying staff** which attacks when touched, a *wand* of *sleep* (25 charges), a *ring of protection +1*, and 10 *potions of inflict serious wounds.*

Flying Staff   **CR 2**
XP 600
hp 21 (Appendix B: New Monsters, "Flying Staff")

Jhedophar keeps spare copies of his spellbooks and his phylactery hidden within a magical chest hidden on the Ethereal Plane using a *secret chest* spell.

Concluding the Adventure

If the characters made a deal with Exeterus and wrested the *mandrake staff* from Jhedophar, they must still return to face the red dragon. They could also try sneaking off with the goods. If the characters did not make a deal with Exeterus, the dragon notices the commotion from the tower and may be lying in wait for the characters when they attempt to leave. It happily extorts any treasure it can get from them as it decides whether to roast and eat them or to let them go.

The adventure concludes when the characters chase off or destroy Jhedophar and Exeterus. It is hoped they made it out with their lives and some new magic items and treasure. This adventure is not about completing some grand quest or accomplishing some great deed. It is about facing down danger and testing one's mettle against dangerous and deadly foes.

Extending the Adventure

Exeterus and Jhedophar are great continuing foes you could use in your ongoing campaign. Perhaps the characters decide to hunt down Jhedophar in the Plane of Molten Skies, or they find themselves stalked by the greedy dragon who uses innocent villagers as hostages as he burns and destroys all in his path to find the characters. This offers various roleplaying opportunities as the heroes are soon regarded as harbingers of doom. The story of villages being destroyed in their passing is passed along on the lips of bards and skalds until the characters finally face up to the threat of Exeterus following them.

Jhedophar might also find the characters an amusing challenge and decide to torment them by popping into their lives from time to time. He might also use the characters to secretly do his dirty work. Jhedophar is extremely intelligent and quite selfishly despicable and unpredictable. Evil or neutral characters may find Jhedophar to be a mentor or powerful patron to their dastardly deeds. Above all, Jhedophar is a survivor and seeks to stay that way.

Characters might also try to uncover the many secrets of the fantastic sword *Karelis.* The weapon seeks a strong hero who may finally free her body from imprisonment on the Plane of Agony.

APPENDIX A: NEW MAGIC

This chapter details new items found in the adventure.

ALCHEMICAL ITEMS

ADHERER OIL

Price 500 gp; **Weight** 1 lb.

Adherer oil is the alchemically distilled secretion of an adherer. This milky glue like substance is very sticky and when applied to a person's body causes the blows of enemies weapons to stick to their body unless their attacker is using a stone weapon or succeeds on a DC 20 Reflex save. Likewise, individuals coated in adherer oil gain a +5 circumstance bonus to any grapple checks they make while thus coated. One application of adherer oil lasts for 3d6 minutes.

Skill Craft (Alchemy) DC 30

MAGIC ITEMS

EYES OF PETRIFICATION

Aura moderate transmutation; **CL** 11th; **Slot** eyes;
Price 98,000 gp; **Weight** —

These items are made of special crystal and fit over the eyes of the wearer. They allow her to use a petrification gaze attack (Fortitude DC 19 negates) for 10 rounds per day. Both lenses must be worn for the magic to be effective.

Feats Craft Wondrous Item, *flesh to stone*; **Cost** 49,000 gp

KARELIS (MINOR ARTIFACT)

Slot none; **CL** 20th; **Weight** 6 lbs.; **Aura** strong enchantment

INTELLIGENT +3 ADAMANTINE BASTARD SWORD

This adamantine longsword is of magnificent craftsmanship, having a suppleness not normally seen in such a weapon. Its chiseled and engraved hilt is done in the ancient elven style of sword dancers, with a green dragon skin wrist thong attached to its star sapphire pommel stone. The emeralds adorning the cross hilt are embedded to appear like a pair of almond-shaped eyes of deep beauty and sadness.

Karelis is neutral good and her powers and abilities may be utilized by any being of good alignment. Karelis has a Charisma of 22, an Intelligence of 20, a Wisdom of 14 and an Ego of 33.

Karelis speaks Abyssal, Celestial, Common, Elven, Sylvan, Infernal, and the secret tongue of the N'gathau*. She is imbued with speech and telepathy.

* Details on the N'gathau are found in *Tome of Horrors Complete* by Frog God Games.

PRIMARY ABILITIES

The primary abilities are:

The wielder of *Karelis* may *detect magic* at will.

The wielder of *Karelis* may *detect evil* as the paladin ability 3/ day.

The wielder of *Karelis* may use *lesser globe of invulnerability* 1 / day.

Karelis may use Sense Motive as if she had 10 ranks of the skill (+12 to Sense Motive checks).

EXTRAORDINARY POWERS

In addition to *Karelis'* primary abilities *Karelis* also possesses the following extraordinary powers:

Deathwatch Dance: Whenever the bearer of *Karelis* drops below 0 hp, *Karelis* animates as a dancing weapon, defending the fallen hero at the hero's base attack bonus for 4 rounds. When this effect takes place the ghostly image of the elf-maiden Karelis appears before the sword bearer's enemies and allies alike as she defends his fallen form although the wounded and unconscious hero may never see this magnificent sight. Should the hero be healed while *Karelis* defends his form, the blade drops to within reach of the hero so that he may again grasp her hilt and rejoin the fight, her image vanishing instantly upon his return to consciousness.

Song of Karelis: Twice per day *Karelis* may be asked to sing her song of battle. This song acts exactly like the bardic ability inspire courage, granting the bearer and his allies a +2 moral bonus to attacks and damage, and a +3 moral bonus to will saves versus charms and fear effects. The lilting elven war-song causes the blade to appear to vibrate, the notes resounding in a 30-foot radius around the bearer of the blade.

INTELLIGENT ITEM PURPOSE

Karelis' special purpose is to destroy the horrid thing her body has become. Although her soul is trapped within her magical blade, the body of *Karelis* lives on in the Plane of Agony. It is now a horrid, twisted, tortured being called a N'Gathau. Neither the soul of *Karelis* or Lord Tork are certain of the truth, but they suspect that Jhedophar sold *Karelis* to demonic creatures called the N'Gathau in exchange for vile wisdom and great power. *Karelis* does not know the new name the N'Gathau have bequeathed to her body, nor does she even know what her body looks like after being twisted and tortured and reshaped by the ghastly rulers of the Plane of Agony. The sword's purpose is to lead heroes appropriate to the task of venturing to the Plane of Agony to find and destroy the N'Gathau that once was *Karelis*, thus allowing her soul escape from the blade and go on to her eternal reward.

While on the Material Plane, her will is to destroy any N'gathau or their minions that she or her wielder comes into contact with.

INTELLIGENT ITEM SPECIAL PURPOSE POWER

When combating a N'gathau, the wielder of Karelis is granted a +3 luck bonus to all saving throws, attack rolls, checks, and AC.

Destruction Should Karelis be used to destroy her original body, the sword loses its intelligence and becomes a normal *+3 Adamantine Bastard Sword*.

MANDRAKE STAFF (MINOR ARTIFACT)

Slot none; **CL** 20th; **Weight** 5 lbs.; **Aura** strong transmutation *+3 / +3 Quarterstaff*

This staff is roughly 6 feet long and nearly 3 inches thick. It is dark and twisted, having the vague appearance of a tortured, withered man. The top of the staff looks like the screaming head of a damned spirit. Legends abound as to the true source of the staff. Whispers and myths speak of a great mandrake root as strong as darkwood dug from beneath the feet of a hanged murderer. It was given life and imbued with magical power by the witches of the Stench-Hollow Downs. Others claim the staff's power is much older. The staff possesses many astounding and deadly qualities and has been sought after by masters of the school of transmutation for its powers of strengthening their magic twofold.

Withering **(2/week).** With a successful melee touch attack with this staff against creatures of up to large size causes a random portion of the body so touched to wither away unless a successful DC 22 Fortitude save is made.

On a failed save, limbs drop off, and in the event of a strike to the head being the result is instant death. A strike to the victims torso causes 2d6 points of constitution drain on a failed save. On a successful Fort save, limbs become useless causing the victim to take 1d6 points of dexterity drain, on a strike to the head the victim takes 1d6 points of charisma drain, and 1d6 points of constitution drain should the blow strike the victim in the torso. The limbs or ability damage may only be recovered with *wish, miracle,* or removal of the limb and subsequent casting of *regeneration.* In the event of death only a *true resurrection* spell may raise a victim thus slain. To determine where the withering strike lands, roll 1d6 and consult the following: 1-head, 2-right arm, 3-left arm, 4-right leg, 5-left leg, 6-torso.

Poison (**1/day**). As *poison* except arcane. Only arcane spellcasters use this feature.

Empowered Transmutation. Anyone with access to the Transmutation school of magic is treated as though they have the feat Spell Focus (Transmutation). Any arcane caster without access to this school may access it while holding this staff.

Spells. You may use the staff to cast one of the following spells, requiring no material components:

3/day: *blink*
2/day: *passwall*
1/day: *flesh to stone, etherealness, plane shift*

Walk of the Mandrake. Once per week, the staff may be commanded to animate and walk about on its own accord for up to 1 hour. The staff sprouts a pair of root-like legs that allow it a movement rate of 30 feet. The staff has an Armor Class of 30, hardness 5, 32 hit points, and attacks with your bonus to hit. While the staff is moving independently of its master, it may use any of its special abilities as long as those special abilities have not gone beyond their allocated number of uses. Destroying it in this form is the only way to destroy the staff. You may use a free action to end this function and return the staff immediately to your hand.

Destruction To destroy the Mandrake Staff, you must slay it while it is using *Walk of the Mandrake.*

Mirror of Charming

Aura moderate enchantment; **CL** 7th; **Slot** —; **Price** 12,000 gp;
  Weight 50 lbs.

This ornate polished silver mirror is bordered in an intricately worked golden frame, making it appear much like a boudoir mirror. It is roughly five feet tall by three feet wide, affording anyone gazing into it a nearly full length view of themselves. Upon gazing into the mirror the viewer must succeed on a DC 20 Will save or become enraptured by their own appearance, unable to leave off looking at themselves. Attempting to remove a viewer from gazing upon the mirror causes the viewer to succeed on a second DC 20 Will save or become enraged as the *rage* spell for 1d6 rounds, attacking anyone who disturbs their viewing.

Feats Craft Wondrous Item, *charm monster, rage*; **Cost** 6,000 gp

Scroll Case of Obscuring

Aura moderate abjuration; **CL** 11th; **Slot** —; **Price** 2,000 gp;
  Weight 2 lbs.

You may store up to five scrolls of any kind within this innocuous looking scroll case's ebon-wood compartment. The scroll case is continually under the effects of a *obscure object* spell. Also, it does not radiate magic for purposes of a *detect magic* spell, regardless of its contents. So would-be thieves using scrying devices and magic will be more likely to ignore the scroll case's presence.

Feats Craft Wondrous Item, *obscure object, permanent image*;
Cost 1,000 gp

Appendix B: New Monsters

Exeteris

Exeteris   CR 15
XP 51,200
CE Huge dragon (fire)
Init +4; **Senses** dragon senses, smoke vision; Perception +25;
    Aura fire aura (5-ft., 1d6 fire), frightful presence (210-ft.,
    DC 22)

AC 32, touch 8, flat-footed 32 (+24 natural, -2 size)
hp 237 (19d12+114)
Fort +17, **Ref** +11, **Will** +16
DR 10/magic; **Immune** fire, paralysis, sleep; **SR** 26
Weaknesses vulnerability to cold

Speed 40 ft., fly 200 ft. (poor)
Melee bite +28 (2d8+16/19-20), 2 claws +28 (2d6+11), 2 wings
    +26 (1d8+5), tail slap +26 (2d6+16)
Space 15 ft.; **Reach** 10 ft. (15 ft. with bite)
Special Attacks breath weapon (50-ft. cone, 14d10 fire
    damage, Reflex DC 25 half, usable every 1d4 rounds), crush
    (Small creatures, DC 25, 2d8+16)
Spell-Like Abilities (CL 19th; concentration +22)
At will—*detect magic, pyrotechnics* (DC 15), *suggestion* (DC 16)
Spells Known (CL 9th; concentration +12)
4th (4/day)—*charm monster* (DC 17), *scrying* (DC 17)
3rd (7/day)—*dispel magic, displacement, slow* (DC 16)
2nd (7/day)—*ghoul touch* (DC 15), *invisibility, shatter* (DC 15),
    web (DC 15)
1st (7/day)—*burning hands* (DC 14), *charm person* (DC 14),
    identify, shield, silent image (DC 14)
0th (at will)—*dancing lights, detect magic, disrupt undead* (DC
    13), *ghost sound* (DC 13), *light, mage hand, prestidigitation,*
    read magic

Str 33, **Dex** 10, **Con** 23, **Int** 16, **Wis** 17, **Cha** 16
Base Atk +19; **CMB** +32; **CMD** 42 (46 vs. trip)
Feats Cleave, Greater Vital Strike, Improved Critical (bite),
    Improved Initiative, Improved Iron Will, Improved Vital
    Strike, Iron Will, Multiattack, Power Attack, Vital Strike
Skills Appraise +25, Bluff +25, Fly +14, Intimidate +25,
    Knowledge (arcana) +25, Perception +25, Sense Motive +25,
    Spellcraft +25, Stealth +14
Languages Common, Draconic, Dwarven, Orc

Special Abilities

Fire Aura (Su) An adult (or older) red dragon is surrounded by an
aura of intense heat. All creatures within 5 feet take 1d6 points of fire
damage at the beginning of the dragon's turn.

Smoke Vision (Ex) A very young (or older) red dragon can see
perfectly in smoky conditions (such as those created by pyrotechnics).

Flying Staff

Flying Staff   CR 2
XP 600
N Small construct
Init +1; **Senses** darkvision 60 ft., low-light vision;
    Perception -5

AC 16, touch 12, flat-footed 15 (+1 Dex, +4 natural, +1 size)
hp 21 (2d10+10)
Fort +0, **Ref** +1, **Will** -5

Defensive Abilities hardness 5; **Immune** construct traits

Speed 30 ft., fly 30 ft. (clumsy)
Melee slam +5 (1d4+3)

Str 14, **Dex** 12, **Con** —, **Int** —, **Wis** 1, **Cha** 1
Base Atk +2; **CMB** +3; **CMD** 14
Skills Fly -5

Ghoul, Minotaur

Minotaur Ghoul   CR 4
XP 1,200
CE Large undead (monstrous humanoid)
Init +2; **Senses** darkvision 60 ft.; Perception +15

AC 18, touch 11, flat-footed 16 (+2 Dex, +7 natural, -1 size)
hp 27 (6d8)
Fort +4, **Ref** +7, **Will** +7
Defensive Abilities channel resistance +2; **Immune** undead
    traits

Speed 30 ft.
Melee bite +5 (1d8+2 plus disease), 2 claws +10 (1d8+5), gore
    +10 (1d6+5)
Space 10 ft.; **Reach** 10 ft.
Special Attacks ghoul fever, paralysis (1d4+1 rounds, DC 13),
    powerful charge (gore, 2d6+7)

Str 21, **Dex** 14, **Con** —, **Int** 9, **Wis** 14, **Cha** 10
Base Atk +6; **CMB** +12 (+14 bull rush); **CMD** 24 (26 vs. bull
    rush)
Feats Great Fortitude, Improved Bull Rush, Power Attack
Skills Intimidate +9, Perception +15, Stealth +4, Survival +12;
    Racial Modifiers +4 Perception, +4 Survival
Languages Giant
SQ natural cunning

Special Abilities

Disease (DC 13) (Su) Ghoul Fever: Bite—injury; save Fort DC
13; onset 1 day; frequency 1/day; effect 1d3 Con and 1d3 Dex; cure 2
consecutive saves. The save DC is Charisma-based.

Natural Cunning (Ex) Although minotaurs are not especially
intelligent, they possess innate cunning and logical ability. This gives
them immunity to maze spells and prevents them from ever becoming
lost. Further, they are never caught flat-footed.

Paralysis (1d4+1 rounds, DC 13) Attacks paralyze foes.

Powerful Charge (Gore, 2d6+7) (Ex) Your charge attacks deal
additional damage.

Golem, Wood Shield Guardian

Wood Shield Guardian Golem   CR 8
XP 4,800
N Medium construct
Init +3; **Senses** darkvision 60 ft., low-light vision; Perception +3

AC 19, touch 13, flat-footed 16 (+3 Dex, +6 natural)
hp 64 (8d10+20); fast healing 5
Fort +2, **Ref** +5, **Will** +5
DR 5/adamantine; **Immune** construct traits, magic
Weaknesses vulnerability to fire

Speed 30 ft.
Melee 2 slams +12 (2d6+4)
Special Attacks splintering
Spell-Like Abilities (CL 8th; concentration +3)—spell storing

Str 18, **Dex** 17, **Con** —, **Int** —, **Wis** 17, **Cha** 1
Base Atk +8; **CMB** +12; **CMD** 25
SQ controlled, find master, guard, shield other

Special Abilities

Controlled (Ex) A shield guardian that has the berserk special attack cannot go berserk as long as the wearer of its amulet is within 30 feet.

Find Master (Su) As long as a shield guardian and its amulet are on the same plane, the shield guardian can locate the amulet's wearer (or just the amulet, if it is removed after the guardian is called).

Guard (Ex) If ordered to do so, a shield guardian moves to defend the wearer of its amulet. All attacks against the amulet wearer take a –2 penalty when the shield guardian is adjacent to its master.

Immunity to Magic (Ex) A wood golem is immune to any spell or spell-like ability that allows spell resistance, with the exception of spells and spell-like abilities that have the Fire descriptor, which affect it normally. In addition, certain spells and effects function differently against the creature, as noted below.

• *Warp wood* or *wood shape* slows a wood golem (as the slow spell) for 2d6 rounds (no save).

• *Repel wood* drives the golem back 60 feet and deals 2d12 points of damage to it (no save).

• A magical attack that deals cold damage breaks any slow effect on the golem and heals 1 point of damage for every 3 points of damage the attack would otherwise deal. If the amount of healing would cause the golem to exceed its full normal hit points, it gains any excess as temporary hit points. A wood golem gets no saving throw against attacks that deal cold damage.

Shield Other (Sp) The wearer of a shield guardian's amulet can activate this defensive ability as a standard action if within 100 feet of the shield guardian. Just as the spell of the same name, this ability transfers to the shield guardian half the damage that would be dealt to the amulet wearer (note that this ability does not provide the spell's AC or save bonuses). Damage transferred in this manner bypasses any defensive abilities (such as immunity or damage reduction) the golem possesses.

Spell Storing (Sp) A shield guardian can store one spell of 4th level or lower that is cast into it by another creature. It "casts" this spell when commanded to do so or when a predefined situation arises. Once this spell is used, the shield guardian can store another spell (or the same spell again).

Splintering (1/1d4+1 rounds, DC 14) (Su) As a free action once every 1d4+1 rounds, a wood golem can launch a barrage of razor-sharp wooden splinters from its body in a 20-foot-radius burst. All creatures caught within this area take 6d6 points of slashing damage (Reflex DC 14 halves). The save DC is Constitution-based.

Grytis

Grytis   **CR 7**
XP 3,200
Advanced giant margoyle
CE Large monstrous humanoid (earth)
Init +3; **Senses** darkvision 60 ft., low-light vision; Perception +14

AC 23, touch 12, flat-footed 20 (+3 Dex, +11 natural, -1 size)
hp 87 (6d10+54)
Fort +10, **Ref** +8, **Will** +8
DR 10/magic

Speed 40 ft., fly 60 ft. (average)

Melee bite +12 (1d8+7), 2 claws +12 (1d8+7), gore +12 (1d8+7)
Space 10 ft.; **Reach** 10 ft.

Str 25, **Dex** 17, **Con** 27, **Int** 12, **Wis** 16, **Cha** 12
Base Atk +6; **CMB** +14; **CMD** 27
Feats Power Attack, Skill Focus (Fly), Toughness
Skills Acrobatics +3 (+7 to jump), Fly +13, Intimidate +10, Perception +14, Stealth +10 (+16 stony environs), Survival +12; **Racial Modifiers** +2 Perception, +2 Stealth (+8 Stealth in stony environs)
Languages Common, Draconic, Terran
SQ freeze

Special Abilities

Freeze (Ex) A gargoyle can hold itself so still it appears to be a statue. A gargoyle that uses freeze can take 20 on its Stealth check to hide in plain sight as a stone statue.

Imbo the Undying

Imbo the Undying   **CR 13**
XP 25,600
Dwarf slayer 14
CE Medium humanoid (dwarf)
Init +2; **Senses** darkvision 60 ft.; Perception +17 (+19 to notice unusual stonework)

AC 21, touch 13, flat-footed 18 (+8 armor, +2 Dex, +1 dodge)
hp 133 (14d10+56); shall know no rest
Fort +12, **Ref** +11, **Will** +4 (+2 bonus vs. detect thoughts, discern lies, and similar mind-reading magic); +2 vs. poison, spells, and spell-like abilities
Defensive Abilities defensive training, evasion, trap sense +4

Speed 20 ft.
Melee *dwarven thrower* +20/+15/+10 (1d8+8/×3), +1 handaxe +18/+13/+8 (1d6+6/×3) or *dwarven thrower* +22/+17/+12 (1d8+8/×3) or +1 handaxe +20/+15/+10 (1d6+6/×3)
Special Attacks hatred, quarry, slayer's advance 1/day, sneak attack +4d6, studied target +3 (3 at a time, swift action)

Str 20, **Dex** 15, **Con** 16, **Int** 10, **Wis** 10, **Cha** 12
Base Atk +14; **CMB** +19; **CMD** 32 (36 vs. bull rush, 36 vs. trip)
Feats Cleave, Cleaving Finish, Dodge, Double Slice, Great Cleave, Greater Two-weapon Fighting, Improved Cleaving Finish, Improved Two-weapon Fighting, Power Attack, Two-weapon Fighting
Skills Acrobatics +18 (+14 to jump), Appraise +0 (+2 to assess nonmagical metals or gemstones), Bluff +20, Disable Device +25, Disguise +3, Perception +17 (+19 to notice unusual stonework), Sense Motive +17, Stealth +18; **Racial Modifiers** +2 Appraise to assess nonmagical metals or gemstones, +2 Perception to notice unusual stonework
Languages Common, Dwarven
SQ combat style (two-weapon combat), slayer talents (assassinate [DC 17], evasion, foil scrutiny, ranger combat style, ranger combat style, ranger combat style, trapfinding), stalker, swift tracker, track +7, trapfinding +7
Other Gear *+2 mithral breastplate, +1 handaxe, dwarven thrower, belt of giant strength +4, headband of alluring charisma +2, ring of mind shielding*

Special Abilities

Assassinate (DC 17) (Ex) Can kill unaware foe with a prepared sneak attack (Fort neg).

Shall Know No Rest (Ex) Imbo cannot die. He can be subdued, disintegrated, or even, consumed; however, his life will always, eventually come back. This process takes 1d10 days. After this time Imbo awakens, usually with a burning desire for revenge on those who slayed him.

Slayer's Advance (1/day) (Ex) As a move action, move up to 2x speed (can stealth at -10).

JHEDOPHAR

Jhedophar CR 19

XP 204,800

Male half-elf lich wizard 18

NE Medium undead (augmented humanoid, elf, human)

Init +1; **Senses** darkvision 60 ft., low-light vision; Perception +36

Aura fear (60 ft., DC 25)

AC 29, touch 16, flat-footed 28 (+8 armor, +5 deflection, +1 Dex, +5 natural)

hp 189 (18d6+126)

Fort +17, **Ref** +12, **Will** +21; +2 vs. enchantments

Defensive Abilities channel resistance +4, rejuvenation; DR 15/bludgeoning, 15/magic; **Immune** sleep, cold, electricity, polymorph, undead traits

---

Speed 40 ft.

Melee *the mandrake staff* +11/+6 (1d6+2) or

touch +9 (1d8+9 negative energy plus paralyzing touch)

Special Attacks hand of the apprentice (12/day), paralyzing touch (DC 25)

Wizard Spells Prepared (CL 18th; concentration +27)

9th—*imprisonment* (DC 28), *meteor swarm* (DC 30), *time stop*

8th—*horrid wilting* (DC 27), *maze, symbol of insanity* (DC 27), *trap the soul*

7th—*delayed blast fireball* (DC 30), *finger of death* (DC 26), *insanity* (DC 26), *prismatic spray* (DC 28)

6th—*acid fog, chain lightning* (DC 27), *contingency, geas/quest, mass suggestion* (DC 25)

5th—*baleful polymorph* (DC 25), *cone of cold* (DC 26), *dominate person* (DC 24), *hold monster* (DC 24), *magic jar* (DC 24), *mind fog* (DC 24)

4th—2x *bestow curse* (DC 23), *charm monster* (DC 23), *dimension door, enervation, phantasmal killer* (DC 23)

3rd—*blink, dispel magic, displacement, haste, magic circle against chaos, protection from energy*

2nd—*blindness/deafness* (DC 21), *blur, invisibility, mirror image, resist energy, web* (DC 21)

1st—*burning hands* (DC 22), *charm person* (DC 20), *magic missile, ray of enfeeblement* (DC 20), *reduce person* (DC 21), *shield, shocking grasp*

0 (at will)—*detect magic, mage hand, mending, read magic*

Str 8, **Dex** 12, **Con** —, **Int** 29, **Wis** 21, **Cha** 22

Base Atk +9; **CMB** +8; **CMD** 24

Feats Combat Casting, Craft Staff, Empower Spell, Forge Ring, Greater Spell Focus (evocation), Greater Spell Penetration, Maximize Spell, Quicken Spell, Scribe Scroll, Skill Focus (Spellcraft), Spell Focus (evocation), Spell Focus (transmutation), Spell Penetration, Spell Perfection (delayed blast fireball), Weapon Focus (touch)

Skills Acrobatics +1 (+5 to jump), Craft (alchemy) +30, Knowledge (arcana) +30, Knowledge (dungeoneering) +21, Knowledge (engineering) +21, Knowledge (geography) +21, Knowledge (history) +21, Knowledge (local) +21, Knowledge (nature) +21, Knowledge (nobility) +21, Knowledge (planes) +30, Knowledge (religion) +21, Linguistics +30, Perception +36, Profession (teacher) +26, Sense Motive +13, Spellcraft +36, Stealth +9; **Racial Modifiers** +10 Perception, +8 Sense Motive, +8 Stealth

Languages Aboleth, Abyssal, Aklo, Aquan, Auran, Azhar, Celestial, Common, Daemonic, Draconic, Dwarven, Elder Thing, Elven, Encephalon Gorger, Gnome, Halfling, High Boros, Ignan, Infernal, Khemitian, Loquatia Arcana, Necronomus, Norsk, Protean, Semuric, Sylvan, Terran, Undercommon, Yithian

SQ arcane bond (*the mandrake staff*), elf blood, metamagic mastery (6/day)

Combat Gear *scroll of disintegrate, scroll of flesh to stone, stone to flesh, scroll of meteor swarm, scroll of prismatic spray, scroll of temporal stasis, scroll of wall of iron;* **Other Gear** *the mandrake staff, boots of striding and springing, bracers of armor +8, cloak of resistance +5, headband of mental superiority +6, iron bands of binding, ring of protection +5, Golden Circlet of Skeleton Warrior Lord Tork*

Special Abilities

Fear Aura (DC 25) Foes in 60 ft are frightened (below 5 HD) or shaken for 18 rds (Will neg).

Hand of the Apprentice (12/day) (Su) As a standard action, throw melee weapon (use Int instead of Dex) and instantly returns.

Metamagic Mastery (6/day) (Su) Spend 1 use per spell level increase to apply a known metamagic feat for free.

Spell Perfection (Delayed Blast Fireball) The selected spell can have 1 metamagic feat applied for free, as long as the modified level stays at or below 9. Double the effects of feats like spell focus, weapon focus [ray], etc. on this spell.

LARTUGI

Lartugi CR 10

XP 9,600

Halfling unchained rogue 11

CE Small humanoid (halfling)

Init +8; **Senses** Perception +20

AC 20, touch 16, flat-footed 15 (+4 armor, +4 Dex, +1 dodge, +1 size)

hp 72 (11d8+22)

Fort +5, **Ref** +14, **Will** +4; +2 vs. fear

Defensive Abilities danger sense +3, evasion, improved uncanny dodge

---

Speed 20 ft.

Melee +1 short sword +12/+12/+7/+7 (1d4+5/19-20) or

+1 short sword +14/+9 (1d4+5/19-20)

Special Attacks sneak attack +6d6

Str 10, **Dex** 19, **Con** 13, **Int** 14, **Wis** 10, **Cha** 10

Base Atk +8; **CMB** +7; **CMD** 22

Feats Alertness, Dodge, Improved Initiative, Improved Two-weapon Fighting, Lightning Reflexes, Two-weapon Fighting, Weapon Finesse

Skills Acrobatics +20 (+16 to jump), Appraise +16, Bluff +14, Climb +2, Diplomacy +14, Disable Device +25, Escape Artist +18, Perception +20, Sense Motive +18, Sleight of Hand +18, Stealth +22; **Racial Modifiers** +2 Acrobatics, +2 Climb, +2 Perception

Languages Common, Dwarven, Elven, Halfling

SQ debilitating injury: bewildered, debilitating injury: disoriented, debilitating injury: hampered, rogue talents (bleeding attack +6, fast stealth, hide in plain sight, ledge

walker, surprise attacks), trapfinding +5
Combat Gear *potion of haste*; **Other Gear** *+1 studded leather, +1 short sword, +1 short sword,* masterwork thieves' tools

Special Abilities

Bleeding Attack +6 (Ex) Sneak attacks also deal 6 bleed damage/round.

Debilitating Injury: Bewildered -2/-6 (Ex) Foe who takes sneak attack damage takes AC pen (more vs. striker) for 1 rd.

Debilitating Injury: Disoriented -2/-6 (Ex) Foe who takes sneak attack damage takes attack pen (more vs. striker) for 1 rd.

Debilitating Injury: Hampered (Ex) Foe who takes sneak attack damage has speed halved (and can't 5 ft step) for 1 rd.

Fast Stealth (Ex) Move at full speed while using the Stealth skill at no penalty.

Hide in Plain Sight (Favored Terrain [Urban]) (Ex) In your selected terrain, you can use Stealth to hide, even while being observed.

Improved Uncanny Dodge (Lv >= 15) (Ex) Retain DEX bonus to AC when flat-footed. You cannot be flanked unless the attacker is Level 15+.

Ledge Walker (Ex) No Acrobatics penalty at full speed on narrow, uneven, or slippery surfaces & not flat footed.

Surprise Attacks +5 (Ex) In surprise round, foes always flat-footed and add bonus sneak attack dam.

LORD TORK

Lord Tork   **CR 17**
XP 102,400
Human skeleton warrior fighter 16
LE Medium undead (augmented humanoid, human)
Init +6; **Senses** darkvision 60 ft.; Perception +6
Aura fear (30 ft., DC 12)

AC 34, touch 13, flat-footed 31 (+12 armor, +2 Dex, +1 dodge, +4 natural, +5 shield)
hp 120 (16d10+32)
Fort +12, **Ref** +7, **Will** +5 (+4 vs. fear)
DR 10/bludgeoning and magic; **Immune** channel energy, undead traits; **SR** 31

Speed 40 ft.
Melee *Karelis* +32/+27/+22/+17 (1d10+17/17-20)
Special Attacks weapon trainings (heavy blades +3, bows +2, light blades +1)

Str 28, **Dex** 14, **Con** — (14), **Int** 10, **Wis** 10, **Cha** 14
Base Atk +16; **CMB** +25 (+27 sunder); **CMD** 38 (40 vs. sunder)
Feats Cleave, Cleaving Finish, Dodge, Exotic Weapon Proficiency (bastard sword), Great Cleave, Improved Cleaving Finish, Improved Critical (bastard sword), Improved Initiative, Improved Sunder, Mobility, Mounted Combat, Point-Blank Shot, Power Attack, Precise Shot, Spring Attack, Surprise Follow-through, Weapon Focus (bastard sword), Weapon Specialization (bastard sword)
Skills Acrobatics +15 (+19 to jump), Climb +11, Handle Animal +21, Intimidate +29, Perception +6, Ride +19, Sense Motive +6; **Racial Modifiers** +8 Intimidate, +6 Perception, +6 Sense Motive
Languages Common
SQ armor training 4, find target
Combat Gear *necklace of fireballs iv;* **Other Gear** *+3 full plate, +3 heavy steel shield, Karelis, belt of giant strength +4, boots of striding and springing*

Special Abilities

Cleave If you hit a foe, attack an adjacent target at the same attack bonus but take -2 AC.

Cleaving Finish Make additional attack if opponent is knocked out

Fear Aura (30 feet, DC 12) Foes within radius are affected by the fear spell.

Find Target (Sp) A skeleton warrior can track and find the possessor of its circlet unerringly, as though guided by discern location. Using this ability, it can also find the last person to possess its circlet. Its caster level is equal to its total Hit Dice.

Improved Cleaving Finish May use Cleaving Finish any number of times/round

Improved Sunder You don't provoke attacks of opportunity when sundering.

Mobility +4 to AC vs. AoO provoked by moving out of or through a threatened area.

Power Attack -5/+10 You can subtract from your attack roll to add to your damage.

Spring Attack You can move - attack - move when attacking with a melee weapon.

Surprise Follow-Through When you are using Cleave, your second foe is denied its Dex bonus.